This
Annual belongs to

_____

ANNUAL 2010

First published in Great Britain 2009 by Egmont UK
Limited, 239 Kensington High Street, London, W8 6SA

Fireman Sam © 2009 Prism Art & Design Limited, a HIT
Entertainment company. The Fireman Sam name and
characters are trademarks. Based on an idea by
D. Gingell, D. Jones and characters created by R. M. J. Lee.

ISBN 978 1 4052 4636 1
10 9 8 7 6 5 4 3 2 1
Printed in Italy

Contents

Meet Fireman Sam

Great Fires of London!

Good morning, Sam! Thanks for answering our questions today. People are really excited to hear what you think!

Well, thank you very much. I'm pleased to be able to help.

So, Sam, when you're not firefighting, what's your favourite hobby?

That would have to be inventing things. I like a bit of time in my shed.

What would you most like to invent?

Well, now, let's see. Probably something that would stop fires from starting.

Do you have any safety tips for the readers?

Yes – don't play near hot cookers or fires and heaters. And if you smell smoke, shout for a grown-up.

Finally, Sam, what are you doing with the rest of your day off?

I'm looking after my niece and nephew, Sarah and James. We're off now to play in the park. Bye then!

Bye, Sam, and thank you! And look out for more fire safety tips on page 34.

The Firefighters

Elvis Cridlington loves rock 'n' roll. He also likes firefighting, and thinks that Fireman Sam is brilliant and Penny is lovely.

Rock 'n' roll!

Penny Morris drives Venus, the red rescue tender. She and Tom have the same hobbies and like the great outdoors.

Go, girl, go!

Station Officer Steele is in charge of the Pontypandy Fire Station. He insists that 'rules are rules' and aren't meant to be broken.

Right, let's go!

Tom Thomas is a daring helicopter pilot from Australia. He's in charge of the Mountain Rescue Station near the base of Pontypandy Mountain.

G'day!

Friends and Family

Dilys and Norman Price. Dilys runs the Pontypandy shop. Her son, 'Naughty' Norman doesn't help much. He prefers playing out with Mandy and causing lots of mischief.

Norman is in trouble again!

Wait 'til I get you home!

The Flood Family. Mike is the local handyman. Helen is a nurse and is great in any emergency. Mandy is Norman's best friend, and a bit of a tomboy.

The Jones Family. Charlie, the fisherman, is Fireman Sam's brother. He and Bronwyn have twins, Sarah and James who love spending time with their Uncle Sam.

Mmm, tea!

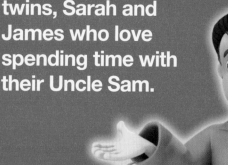

Trevor Evans drives the local bus, taking the children to school and keeping the local people on the move. He enjoys a good gossip over a cup of tea.

Cool!

A Wish Come True

Bronwyn has taken Sarah and James for a walk.

Look! Lion has come too!

The children find an old well.

Cool!

Bronwyn gives them coins to make a wish.

Hello! Is anybody there?!

That's silly. How can a well make a wish come true?

I wish I didn't have to walk home.

Lion is being a naughty cat, and chasing birds.

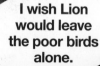

I wish Lion would leave the poor birds alone.

Meanwhile, Tom is in his helicopter.

Come in, Sam! I think we need you.

The firefighters soon arrive at the well.

Look, it's Uncle Sam!

Meanwhile, Lion is still up to no good.

One pounce and I can reach you.

Sam puts out the fire.

Looks like somebody had a barbecue up here and didn't put it out properly.

Sam gives Tom a thumbs up.

Phew! All under control again.

James has an idea to make his wish come true ...

Well, I guess so!

Hi, Uncle Sam! Can I ride back with you?

Dino Prints

Norman has made dinosaur prints with his giant stamper. Which of the stampers here makes the correct footprint shape?

1

2

3

4

5

6

Answer on page 68.

Mountain Rescue

Here's Tom Thomas in his super rescue helicopter!
Look carefully at the 4 circles. Which circle is part of the big picture?
Put a tick (✓) in the box below the correct circle.

a   b   c   d

Answer on page 68.

The Great Outdoors

Norman had had a great idea. He decided to make a tent. He always wanted to go camping.

But his mum wasn't happy. "Norman? What are you doing with my best blanket?"

"Mam, please! I'm going camping in the great outdoors!"

"Norman Price! Outdoors is dirty, cold and dangerous."

Trevor was in Dilys' shop. "Camping, eh, Norman? I used to be a boy scout, you know?"

Wow, Trevor! Did you sleep in a tent and cook on a campfire?

Trevor said he would take Norman camping at the weekend.

"Thanks, Trevor!" said Norman. "That would be brilliant!"

Dilys was excited too, but Norman hadn't planned on his mum going with them!

That weekend, Trevor put up their tents on Pontypandy Mountain. Dilys made a campfire.

"Norman says there are **WILD CATS** around here," said Dilys nervously.

"Don't you worry, Dilys. That's not true!" said Trevor.

ROOOAAARR!!

But then they heard a noise. "Aaaaaaaaaaaaagh!" screamed Dilys. But Trevor wasn't scared. He could see Norman hiding behind a rock. It was his roar they had heard!

"Norman, don't do that to your mother! Now behave yourself, and help us collect some more firewood," he said.

Trevor built a circle of stones around their pile of sticks.

"There we go," he said. "Forest fires are much more dangerous than imaginary wild animals. That's why I've built our campfire so carefully."

Norman joined in. "Yeah! Once some campers didn't realise that the woods were on fire until the flames reached their tents …"

Stop frightening your mother, young man!

Later, as it began to get dark, they sat by the campfire. The flames flickered warmly.

Dilys stood up to gaze at the countryside. Then she saw an orange glow in the trees.

Fire! FOREST FIRE! Norman, Trevor, the trees are on fire!

Trevor tried to get Dilys and Norman safely back to the bus but Dilys panicked and ran the wrong way. She tripped over their pile of extra firewood, knocking the sticks everywhere.

"Help! Call Fireman Sam!"

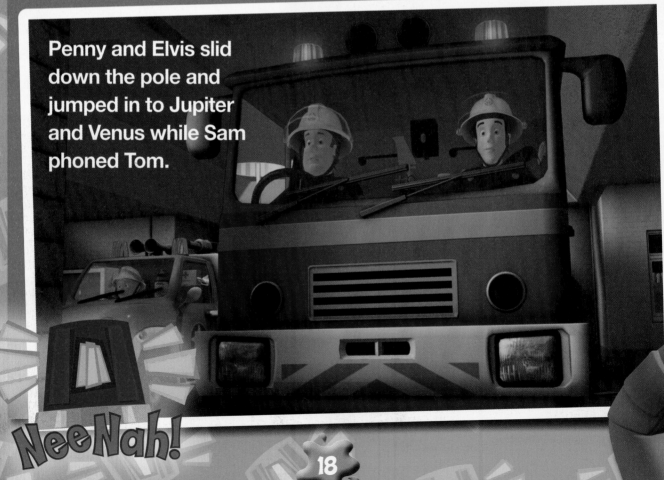

Penny and Elvis slid down the pole and jumped in to Jupiter and Venus while Sam phoned Tom.

NeeNah!

Before they drove to safety, Trevor looked back at the campsite. He couldn't see a forest fire.

"Where was the fire you saw, Dilys?"

Dilys pointed through the trees to where she saw the fire. But there weren't any flames or smoke. Dilys had seen the sunset!

"Norman Price! If you hadn't frightened your mother with your silly stories, this never would have happened! If you're going to behave like this, we might as well go home right now."

Norman was sorry and ashamed.

They called Fireman Sam to explain it was a false alarm. But Tom was checking the area, and he could see smoke coming from the mountain. They were all very confused.

LOOK, FIRE!

Norman went back to the tents. He was very sorry for what he had done. Then he saw the orange flickering of a real fire. The campfire had spread across the sticks and set the tents on fire!

"Call Fireman Sam again now!"

Tom took off in his helicopter to fly towards the smoke he'd seen. Jupiter arrived at the campsite and Sam, Penny and Elvis jumped out.

"Bring the hoses!" shouted Sam. They ran towards the flames, but the hoses were too short. Elvis fell over trying to drag his hose. They couldn't reach the tents to put out the flames!

Luckily, Tom arrived in his helicopter with water tanks. He poured water on to the tents, and the fire quickly went out.

Water on!

Back at the Fire Station, Trevor said sorry to Fireman Sam.

"I should never have left the campfire. Perhaps I'm not a very good boy scout any more."

"That's OK, Trevor," said Sam. "Even boy scouts have accidents sometimes."

Dilys looked out to Norman's new camping site.

"Do you think Norman is safe camping on his own, Sam?"

"Yes, he's quite safe. It's not exactly what he was expecting, though!"

The end.

True or False?

Read the sentence under each picture. Is it true or false?
Draw a ring around the correct answer each time.

1

Sarah is in between James and Norman.

TRUE   FALSE

2

Lion the cat is outside the box.

TRUE   FALSE

3

Lion the cat is on the stool.

TRUE   FALSE

4

Fireman Sam is in front of the dog.

TRUE   FALSE

22

Answers on page 68.

Rhythm Sticks!

Mike Flood has dropped his drumsticks. Can you count how many are in the pile?

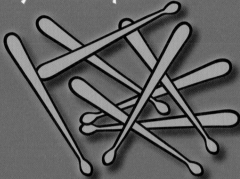

Puzzling Picture

Help Norman by working out which of these jigsaw pieces is missing from the picture.

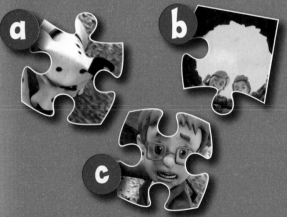

a

b

c

23

Answers on page 68.

Hello, Penny!

Colour in this picture of Penny and Venus. Copy the small picture to make sure you get the colours right!

In the Doghouse

Follow the wiggly lines to see who is going in to which kennel.

Nipper

Lion

Radar

Answers on page 68.

Baa Baa Baby

A cold wind was blowing outside and everyone was feeling the chill. Bronwyn was in the café trying to think warm thoughts.

"I am not **cold** ... I am not cold!" she said over and over.

Charlie had brought an electric heater to help **warm** things up.

"This should keep us cosy until Mike can fix our boiler," he said.

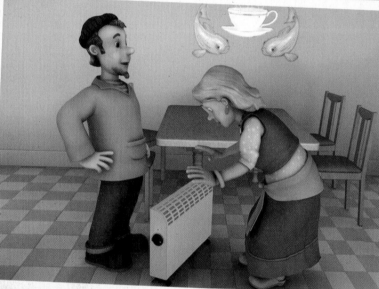

"Just remember, heaters can be

very dangerous!

Don't put anything on top of it – including wet towels. That's how fires start," Charlie warned.

Waaaaah!

Outside Sarah and James were trying to find Norman. They had looked everywhere.

"Wait!" said James as they walked along a quiet road. "Can you hear a baby crying?"

Sarah followed the baby noise. She peeped over a wall and found ...

Norman!

He was with his pet sheep, Woolly, and a little lamb.

"James thought it was a baby!" Sarah laughed.

James was cross. "I did NOT! And if I did so did you ..." he said. The little lamb bleated again. It did sound a lot like a baby.

Sarah had an idea, she thought it would be funny to pretend the lamb was a baby. "Norman, can I borrow your lamb, please?" she asked.

Brrrrrrr!

At the fire station Station Officer Steele was feeling the cold too.

Penny **jogged on the spot**. "If you keep moving, Sir, you stay warm," she said.

Sam smiled. "Not everyone has as much energy as you do, Penny."

Officer Steele was a bit upset. "What do you mean, Sam? I may be a little bit older than you, but I still have lots of energy!" He jogged on the spot like Penny, and then ran into his office. **"I'm as fit as a fiddle! How cheeky!"**

Waaaaah!

Sarah took the lamb to the café. It was now snuggled up in her old doll's pram. She wanted to see how many people would think it was a real baby.

Waaaaah!

Sarah saw Dilys and decided to try her trick. She pushed the pram past Dilys. "Oh, a baby!" smiled Dilys. "Oh! What an unusual face!"

All of a sudden, it started to rain heavily so **Sarah hurried home.** The heater had warmed up the café.

"Poor wet Lambikins! Just let me take off my jumper and I'll get a towel for you."

Sarah popped her *jumper on to the heater* to dry, and went upstairs to fetch a towel.

Suddenly, Sarah heard the smoke alarm beeping. She ran downstairs and saw her jumper had caught fire!

Charlie rushed into the café.

"Quick, call Fireman Sam!

Sarah, come outside! Stand over there where it's safe."

ZZZZZZZ

Station Officer Steele had done too much jogging for one day. He was fast asleep!

Luckily, Sam and the others picked up a message about the fire at the café. Then they *tiptoed* out of Steele's office and climbed into Jupiter.

Arrgh!

Sam arrived at the café. "What's happening?" he asked. "Is anyone inside? Is that a **baby crying**?"

Sarah **gasped**. "I'm sorry, Sam. It's not a baby. It's a lamb. I was looking after it and it's still inside!"

"It's OK, Sarah. We'll take it from here," said Sam. "Penny, Elvis, get the breathing apparatus and the hoses."

Sam soon appeared in the doorway with the lamb safe in his arms. The crowd cheered.

"YEAH! WOO HOO!"

Our Hero

Back at the station, Officer Steele woke with a jump. "Good thing there wasn't an emergency, or somebody would have caught me sleeping on the job! It's very quiet in here. **Where is everybody?!**"

The end.

Double Trouble

Sarah and James can't wait to go skateboarding.
Colour them in before they go!

32

Feed the Birds

Tom Thomas loves birds. Read the questions and draw a circle around the correct answers below.

How many black seeds can you see?

10 12 14 16 18

How many white seeds can you see?

9 11 13 15 17

Starry, Starry Night

Norman was so excited when he saw a **shooting star** on New Year's Eve!

Look carefully at this picture. Can you spot the only star with 4 points?

Answers on page 68.

Fire Safety

Station Officer Steele is giving a safety lesson.
Talk to a grown-up about staying safe if there's a fire.
Can you think of any other safe things to do?

Always remember:

1

Keep toys and clothes away from fires and heaters!

2

Don't play near hot cookers or boiling pots and pans!

3

If you smell smoke, shout for your family and get help!

4

Leave the house and don't go back inside!

Our Heroes

Nothing is too much trouble for Fireman Sam and the crew.
Colour in this picture of them as neatly as you can.

Big and Small

Do you know the difference between **big** and small?
See if you can answer the questions below.

1

Which is smaller, the white sheep or the black sheep?

2

Who is bigger, Dilys or Norman?

3

Which is bigger, the blue and red firework or the yellow and purple firework?

4

Which drum is biggest?

37

Answers on page 68.

Helen Flood has to go away for a few days. Mike and Mandy will be left at home to look after the house.

Mike and Helen are telling Dilys all about it.

It'll be fine. Mandy is very good at helping with the housework.

I wish Norman would help with the chores.

Norman thinks it's time to make a speedy getaway.

Later that afternoon.

Bye, Mum!

Bye, then! Here's a list of jobs that need doing.

It's a very long list!

Elvis is doing his chores at the fire station. He's going to fall down that hole if he's not careful!

But then ...

Ooops!

HELP!

Hold on, Elvis!

Fireman Sam can see Elvis hanging on to his mop.

Norman Price! There are a lot of jobs to do, and I need your help!

Oof!

Nothing broken!

But the mop handle breaks and Elvis falls on top of Sam.

Back at Dilys' shop.

39

40

... and then zooms off before he is given more jobs to do.

Wheeeeeeee!

Elvis visits Dilys.

Morning, Dilys. I need a new mop ...

SHHHHH ... Can you hear a swooshing noise?

Dilys phones for help.

Mike Flood. How can I help?

Oh, Mike, come quickly! Norman has broken the washing machine!

Mike Flood comes to the rescue!

Looks like it was overloaded! I'll have to get a new part before I can fix it.

Later ...

Norman! You broke our washing machine! So now you need to ask Mike very nicely if you can use his machine!

Mandy leaves Norman to sort things out.

Have fun, Norman!

BUT...

NeeNah! NeeNah!

Back at the Floods' house:

Oh no! My iron!

Call Fireman Sam!

42

The firefighters arrive at Mike's house.

Oh no! What's Norman done now?!

It's my fault. I went out and left the iron on.

Bravely, Sam tackles the fire.

Water on!

The fire's out but the Flood's house is still a bit of a state.

Dad, what are we going to tell Mum?

I'm sure she'll be fine. Just don't ask Elvis to mop up the mess!

The end.

Norman's Hobbies

Dilys wants Norman to tidy his bedroom and do the washing. He's in big trouble!

The items below are scattered around Norman's messy bedroom, can you find them?

44

45

Answers on page 68.

Mega Maze

The four rescue vehicles are trying to get to the fire in the middle of the maze. Can you help them all find a way through?

Which vehicle has to go past Norman?

Which vehicle passes the twins?

The Colour of Danger

Elvis was in a *good mood*. He sang his new song as he cooked.

"Red is for danger, Red is what I said, So if you're in danger, The colour is RED!"

He danced around and sang into a wooden spoon like a microphone.

Station Officer Steele followed the smell of cooking. He didn't look very happy.

"**Ahem!** We are not here to sing and dance. We are here to fight fires!" he said.

"Ooh, we certainly are!" shouted Sam, as he spotted their lunch in *flames*.

Nearby, Charlie and Bronwyn were looking after Nipper the dog. He had just buried Charlie's slipper in the sand!

"Aww," said Bronwyn. "He just likes burying things – don't you, Nipper?"

Nipper saw the open door and **zoomed** outside.

He ran into the road, straight in front of **Nurse Flood's** car. Sam heard the noise and hurried out of the station.

Screeech!

"Oh, Nipper!" **puffed** Bronwyn. "I'm sorry, Helen. He's my sister's dog and he's so full of energy!"

Sam handed him to Bronwyn. "I think he needs a **long walk** to tire him out."

"I think you're right, Sam," said Bronwyn. "I'll take him along the cliff path later. I'm so sorry he's caused such **trouble**."

Red is for danger,
Red is what I said,
So if you're in danger,
The colour is RED!

At the café Charlie was making sandwiches to replace the lunch that Elvis had burnt. Elvis sang his new song to the twins. James and Sarah loved it! They clapped and **cheered** loudly.

Charlie made some extra sandwiches to put in a picnic for Bronwyn.

"We're going for a long walk with Nipper, so we'll need a healthy meal," she said.

"Aw, Mum! Walking is **BORING!**" moaned James.

"Well, you come with me," said his dad. "We'll go **fishing** and have our picnic on the boat. Don't forget your phone!" added Charlie, as Bronwyn and Sarah were leaving.

Sarah and Bronwyn were enjoying their walk. "Let's stop here, Mum. We might be able to see Dad and James." They could just make out the boat, and they waved.

Nipper wasn't bothered about what was out at sea. The cheeky dog had found Bronwyn's phone.

Excellent! thought Nipper. Something to bury!

He **bounded** off behind a rock and found a good place to dig.

Bronwyn spread out the picnic blanket and got out their food. She was very hungry. So was Nipper!

"Naughty dog!" shouted Sarah. Nipper ran off and Sarah chased him.

"AAGH!"

Sarah cried in pain. She had tripped over and hurt her leg. It really hurt. She didn't want to cry, so she bit her lip and sat down. She sang Elvis' song quietly, to stop the tears from coming.

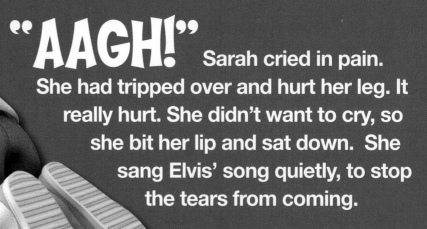

Bronwyn couldn't find her phone. Luckily, she spotted **Fireman Sam** walking on the beach. She jumped up and down and waved.

Sam saw her, and waved back happily. He didn't know that anything was wrong. Bronwyn looked worriedly at Sarah.

"That's it!" shouted Bronwyn. She picked up the red picnic blanket and waved it high in the air. Nipper **barked loudly** and bounced around.

Sam saw Bronwyn's red sign.

"Red is for danger ..." sang Sarah bravely.

"Red is for danger! Something's wrong!"

Brring brring!

Sam tried to ring Bronwyn but her phone just rang and rang.

"Hmm, no answer," said Sam to himself. "I'll call the station and get them to send **Tom** from mountain rescue."

Nipper barked again and then ran back along the cliff.

"Mum!" shouted Sarah. "Nipper's gone!"

WOOF!

"That dog!" cried Bronwyn. "I wish we'd never said we'd take care of him!"

Sarah and Bronwyn both looked up as they heard a helicopter. **It was Tom!**

Bronwyn waved and pointed to Sarah. Tom hovered overhead, but there was nowhere for him to land. He circled round and wondered how he could help.

Nipper ran and reached the road, then dashed straight in front of Nurse Flood's car again.

Nurse Flood was very cross. Every time she got close, Nipper took a few steps back towards the cliff. Nurse Flood had to follow him. She couldn't just leave!

As Nurse Flood reached the cliff top, she could see a group of people. It looked like Fireman Sam.

Screeech!

"Helen! What are you doing here?" asked Bronwyn.

"Nipper brought me! What's going on?"

"Sarah has hurt her leg. We waved at Sam and he climbed up to help us."

Nurse Flood checked Sarah's leg. She thought it was fine, but it needed an **X-ray** to make sure.

Come in, Tom!

Sam called Tom. "We need to get Sarah to hospital."

Tom talked back, loud and clearly. "I can't land, but I can send down a stretcher."

"Super job, Tom. Do your stuff!" Nurse Helen and Sam lifted Sarah carefully.

"Bye, love!" said Bronwyn. "Sam will look after you, and I'll see you at the hospital."

"Well, now, that was a close one!" said Sam later when they were all together again. "Thank goodness for Nipper!"

"And for Elvis!" added Sarah. "It's a good job we knew his song …"

They all joined in and sang the song together.

Red is for danger, Red is what I said, So if you're in danger, The colour is RED!

The end.

Red Alert

Sirens on, Jupiter is ready for action! How alert are you? These 2 pictures may look the same, but 5 things are different in picture 2. Can you spot them all?

Nee Nah!

Nee Nah!

2

There is never a dull moment in Dilys Price's shop! Look at the big picture and see if you can spot each of the things below.

Tick the box next to each item when you have found it.

Cut it Out!

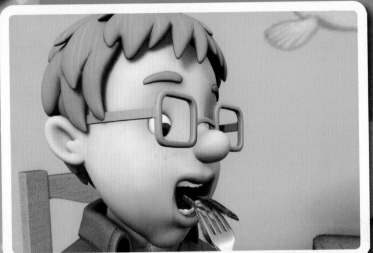

Sarah and James are at the café. They had been collecting mussels to eat. Norman had never tried them before.

"Ew! They're crunchy! Are they cooked?"

The twins giggled. "Norman, that's the shell. Look, you're supposed to eat the soft bit inside!"

Norman liked them. "Did they come from our beach? Can I collect some?"

Hee hee!

Charlie and Bronwyn thought that was a great idea. They got their buckets and promised to set off straight away. The tide had gone out, so the mussels would be left on the rocks.

Elvis was at the station learning how to cut things with the 'jaws of life'.

Sam promised to let Elvis use them the next time they were needed.

Mike Flood was working. "There we go," he said. "Just lean that wood there … and then let's find the paint."

Mike climbed inside the back of his van.

Bang!

Oops! The doors slammed shut and the wood got wedged. Mike was stuck!

"Er – oh. It's a bit dark in here, isn't it? Help! Better call Fireman Sam!"

Help!

Sam and Elvis arrived to rescue Mike. Elvis brought the jaws of life.

"Don't worry, Mike, we'll have you out in no time!"

Sam gently pushed Elvis away. Instead, he moved the wood and opened the doors to let Mike out.

"Sorry, Elvis, but the jaws of life are only for emergencies. We don't need them every time! Ooh, we've got another call. Lion is stuck in a tree again!"

Elvis grabbed the jaws of life and rushed to where Lion was.

Sam looked at him. "Elvis ...?"

Elvis gave a big sigh. He put down the jaws of life and got out a ladder instead. "Sorry, Sam. You're right, of course."

Meanwhile, the children were at the beach. The twins showed Norman how to twist the mussels off the rocks. But Norman was getting impatient. They were collecting **LOADS** more than he was.

Norman wandered off to find more mussels. The rocks were really slippy. **Whoops!** His foot slipped and got stuck. He pulled and pulled but it wouldn't come out. "**HELP!**" he yelled. "Call Fireman Sam!"

Sam and Elvis soon arrived. Elvis had the jaws of life in his hands. He looked at Norman, and then bent down to the water.

"Right, Norman. Let's just untie your shoelace ... can you get your foot out now? Good stuff!"

Elvis helped Norman struggle out of his shoe.

"One more thing!" said Elvis, and this time, he used the jaws of life. "There we go ... your shoe!"

Our Hero

The end.

Rescue Jeep

Answer the questions about Tom Thomas in his jeep.
Put a tick (✓) next to the correct answer each time.

a How many red circles can you count? 2 ☐ 4 ☐ 6 ☐

c How many people are in the truck? 1 ☐ 2 ☐ 4 ☐

b What colour are the 3 lights in a row on the bonnet?
Red ☐ White ☐ Blue ☐

d Count how many red stripes there are on the front.
4 ☐ 5 ☐ 6 ☐ 7 ☐

64

Answers on page 68.

Skate Silhouettes

Can you match the picture of Norman on his skateboard to the correct silhouette?

A

B

C

D

Answer on page 68.

Shape Search

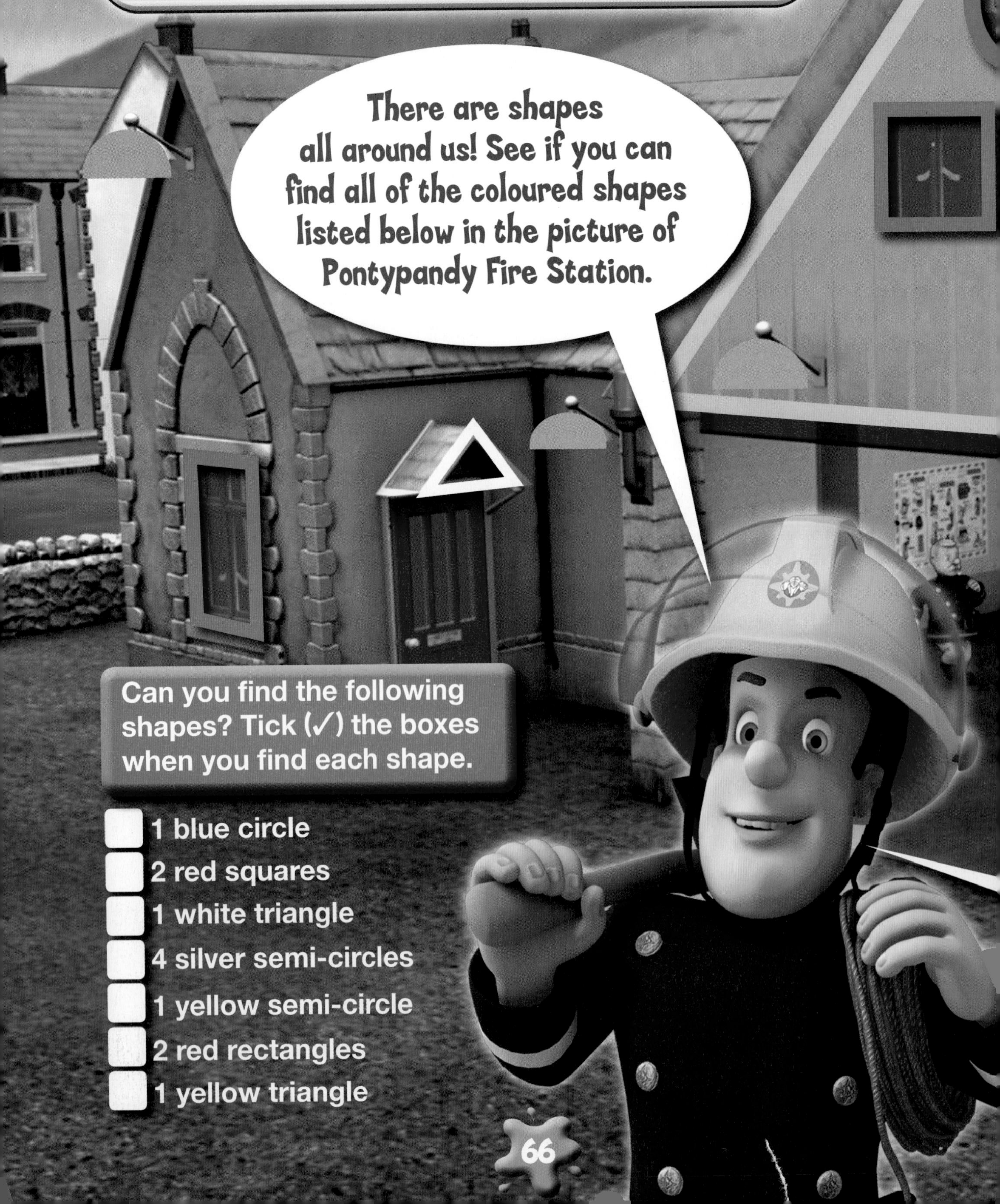

There are shapes all around us! See if you can find all of the coloured shapes listed below in the picture of Pontypandy Fire Station.

Can you find the following shapes? Tick (✓) the boxes when you find each shape.

- [ ] 1 blue circle
- [ ] 2 red squares
- [ ] 1 white triangle
- [ ] 4 silver semi-circles
- [ ] 1 yellow semi-circle
- [ ] 2 red rectangles
- [ ] 1 yellow triangle

66

Goodbye from all
of us in Pontypandy.
We hope to see you
again soon!

Answers on page 68.

Answers

Page 14
Dino Prints
Stamper 5 makes the correct shape

Page 15
Mountain Rescue
The correct circle is d

Page 22
True or False?
1. false 2. false 3. true 4. false

Page 23
Rhythm Sticks!
There are 8 drumsticks

Puzzling Picture
Piece a is missing

Page 25
In the Doghouse
Nipper goes in to kennel 2,
Lion goes in to kennel 1 and
Radar goes in to kennel 3

Page 33
Feed the Birds
There are 14 black seeds and
17 white seeds

Page 33
Starry, Starry Night

Page 37
Big and Small
1. the white sheep. 2. Dilys.
3. the yellow and purple firework.
4. the bottom drum

Page 44
Norman's Hobbies

Page 46
Mega Maze

Nurse Flood's car has to go past
Norman. Tom Thomas' Mountain
Rescue Jeep passes the twins
on its journey to the fire

Page 56
Red Alert

Page 58
I Spy with My Little Eye

Page 64
Rescue Jeep
a. 4 b. white c. 1 d. 7

Page 65
Skate Silhouettes
B is the correct silhouette.

Page 66
Shape Search

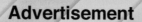